Sam's First Soccer Practice

Preface

Once my children turned three years old, I left my day job to focus on raising them. The journey of seeing them grow up and go through every new experience has been a true blessing. Time has flown by, and I decided to relive those moments by capturing them in book format as first experiences.

The story of Sam's first practice is based on my experience with my two sons. It touches upon the themes of being nervous, teamwork, learning, persistence, encouragement, and having fun! I really hope you enjoy this book and that it helps you develop reading skills in a topic that you enjoy (soccer!).

"Sam the soccer star!"

That's what all the boys in the neighborhood would call him. Wherever he was, Sam always had a soccer ball with him.

Finally it was Sam's big day – his first soccer practice!

Sam hopped in the car with his mom, and they were on their way to soccer practice. After a quick drive, they arrived at the big soccer field.

"Are you ready?" Sam's mom asked.

But Sam did not answer. After seeing all the other boys on the field, he started to feel like his stomach was doing backflips. He was very nervous.

Sam's nerves soon went away when a big man walked up to him.

"Hi, Sam! My name is Coach Ron. Nice to meet you," the man said.

He kindly shook Sam's hand and showed him a warm smile. Sam was now ready to get on the field.

"Pass the ball! Pass the ball!" the other boys screamed.

Sam got upset. He had never played with a team before and didn't understand why teamwork was important.

Then Coach Ron blew the whistle. It was time
to go home.

"How did you like your first soccer practice, Sam?" Mom asked.

Sam was quiet during the entire car ride home. He was not happy, and he did not want to talk.

Sam went to talk to his best friend, Ben. Sam explained how he didn't like soccer practice at all.

"Just give it one more try, Sam! Listen to what coach is teaching you. I know you can do it!" Ben said.

The next day Mom yelled, "Let's go, Sam! We're going to be late!"

Sam quickly put on his uniform and took one last look in the mirror.

"I am Sam the soccer star," he said to himself. He was ready to take on the field again.

Coach Ron taught the team a lot about teamwork that day.

"I know you all want to score a goal, but we need to work together," he said.

When playing with his friends, Sam was always the one who would score a goal. But now he had to learn to share the ball with others as well.

After listening to Coach Ron, Sam finally got a chance to show off his soccer skills.

While he was practicing some dribbling skills, he looked over and waved to his mom and dad, but they were not the only ones there to watch him. Ben was there too!

Sam was very happy that his best friend came to watch him.

When Sam was done with practice, he ran over to Ben.

"That's the soccer player I know!" Ben said and chuckled.

Sam said he liked soccer practice now, and asked Ben to join him. The best friends then went off to practice some more.

If your child enjoyed this story, I would be really grateful if you would PLEASE leave a review. It will inspire me to write more books!

End

Made in United States
North Haven, CT
09 April 2023

35246958R00015